Published by
Delacorte Press
Bantam Doubleday Dell Publishing Group, Inc.
666 Fifth Avenue
New York, New York 10103

This edition was first published by William Collins Sons & Co. Ltd.
Copyright © Nick Butterworth 1991

Library of Congress in Publication Data
Butterworth, Nick.
Amanda's Butterfly / Nick Butterworth.
p. cm.
Summary: While looking for butterflies, a young girl discovers an
even more beautiful winged creature, who needs her help.
ISBN 0-385-30433-1.– ISBN 0-385-30434-X (lib. bdg.)
[1. Fairies–Fiction. 2. Stories without words.] I. Title
PZ7. B98225Am 1991
[E]–dc20   90-48740   CIP   AC

Manufactured in Great Britain.
September 1991
10 9 8 7 6 5 4 3 2 1

AMANDA'S *Butterfly*

NICK BUTTERWORTH

Delacorte Press

For Amanda

When Father Christmas seems too fat
For the chimney,
And you have no more teeth
For the tooth fairy;
There is still some magic in the world
That you can believe in.

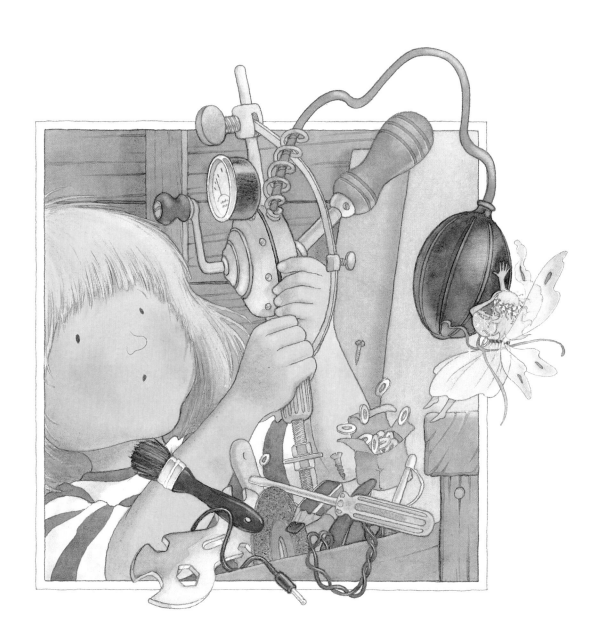

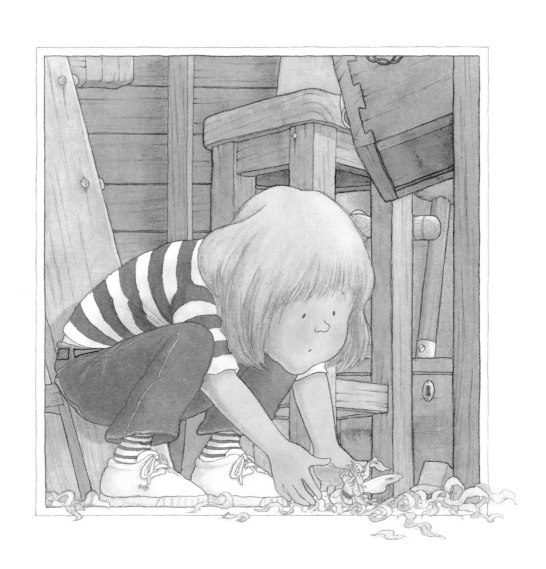

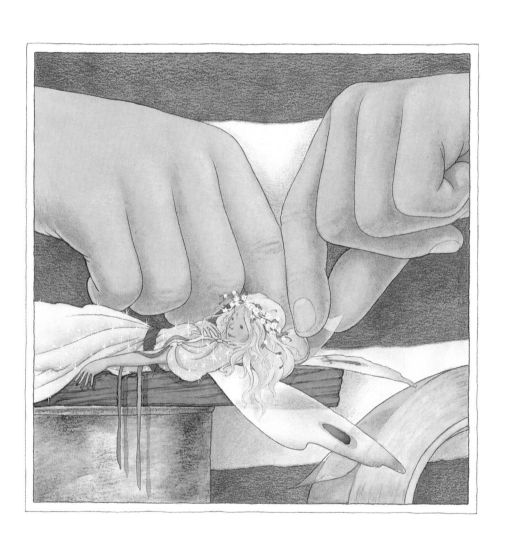